Dear Parent:
Your child's lov̶̶̶̶̶̶̶̶̶̶̶̶̶̶'s here!

Every child learns to read in a different way and at his or her own speed.
You can help your young reader improve and become more confident
by encouraging his or her own interests and abilities. You can also guide
your child's spiritual development by reading stories with biblical values
and Bible stories, like I Can Read! books published by Zonderkidz. From
books your child reads with you to the first books he or she reads alone,
there are I Can Read! books for every stage of reading:

SHARED READING
Basic language, word repetition, and whimsical
illustrations, ideal for sharing with your emergent reader.

BEGINNING READING
Short sentences, familiar words, and simple concepts for
children eager to read on their own.

READING WITH HELP
Engaging stories, longer sentences, and language play
for developing readers.

READING ALONE
Complex plots, challenging vocabulary, and high-interest
topics for the independent reader.

ADVANCED READING
Short paragraphs, chapters, and exciting themes for the
perfect bridge to chapter books.

I Can Read! books have introduced children to the joy of reading since
1957. Featuring award-winning authors and illustrators and a fabulous
cast of beloved characters, I Can Read! books set the standard for
beginning readers.

A lifetime of discovery begins with the magical words **"I Can Read!"**

Visit www.icanread.com for information on enriching your child's reading experience.
Visit www.zonderkidz.com for more Zonderkidz I Can Read! titles.

Diligent hands will rule,
but laziness ends in slave labor.
— Proverbs 12:23–25

ZONDERKIDZ

LarryBoy Meets the Bubblegum Bandit
Copyright© 2011 Big Idea Entertainment, LLC. VEGGIETALES®, character names,
likenesses and other indicia are trademarks of and copyrighted by Big Idea
Entertainment, LLC. All rights reserved.
Illustrations © 2011 by Big Idea Entertainment, LLC.

Requests for information should be addressed to:

Zondervan, *Grand Rapids, Michigan 49530*

Library of Congress Cataloging-in-Publication Data

Poth, Karen
    LarryBoy meets the bubblegum bandit / written by Karen Poth.
        p. cm.
    Based on the video series: Larryboy.
    ISBN 978-0-310-72161-1 (softcover)
    I. Larryboy. II. Title.
PZ7.P83975Lar 2011
[E]—dc22.   2010028326

Editor: Mary Hassinger
Art direction: Karen Poth
Cover design: Karen Poth
Interior design: Ron Eddy

Printed in China

18 19 /DSC/ 21 20 19 18 17 16 15 14 13 12 11 10

ZONDERkidz

I Can Read!

BEGINNING
READING

1

LarryBoy Meets The Bubblegum Bandit

story by Karen Poth

One day, Mayor Blueberry
saw something strange.
The Bumblyburg Elementary
School was a mess!

She tried to find the janitor.

But all she found were mops

hanging in the closet.

When she found the janitor, he was
just standing in the messy hall.
"Something must be wrong,"
Mayor Blueberry thought.

The halls were a mess.

There was gum stuck to the walls.

But she could not be late.

She was going to a big swim meet.

Outside, Mayor Blueberry

saw Spud, the yard boy.

His mower was not mowing.

His rake was not raking.

Spud was lying in a hammock.

He was reading a book

and chewing gum.

"Something must be wrong,"

thought Mayor Blueberry again.

At the pool, the swim team was
not ready for the meet.

They were not even in the pool.

"We don't feel like swimming
today," said Laura Carrot.

Something was very wrong.

The whole town was lazy!

Mayor Blueberry called LarryBoy.

RING, RING!

At the LarryBoy mansion,

Alfred answered the phone.

"Master Larry, it's the mayor.

There is an outbreak

of laziness in the city."

LarryBoy did not hear Alfred.

He was reading a comic book

and eating a donut.

He was dropping crumbs

on the floor. What a mess!

In fact, his whole room was a mess.
LarryBoy's clothes and toys
were everywhere.

"Master Larry, what are you doing?

Bumblyburg needs you!"

Alfred said.

"Oh, Alfred," LarryBoy said.

"I just don't feel like being

a superhero today."

"Master Larry," said Alfred,

"God doesn't want us to be lazy."

"Oh, okay, Alfred," LarryBoy said.

But his super suit was as

big a mess as his room.

Alfred pulled a hanger off

LarryBoy's back.

"Master Larry," he said,

"this hanger is stuck with … gum!"

"Oh, yeah," LarryBoy said.
"I got this jar of golden gum balls
from my new friend, Bubba."

"Have some," LarryBoy continued.

"They're yummy!"

Looking wrinkled and torn,

LarryBoy jumped into the Larrymobile

and headed to the mayor's office.

While he was gone, Alfred grabbed the
gum and got to work on his computer.

When LarryBoy got to the

mayor's office, Bubba was there.

He brought some gum balls for

the mayor, the police chief,

and Editor Bob too!

"Would you like a gum ball?"

Bubba asked politely.

As LarryBoy took the gum,

Alfred burst through the door.

"Spit out your gum!" Alfred shouted.

"Oh, Alfred," LarryBoy said,

"I didn't get the flavor out yet."

"LarryBoy, this is serious!"

Alfred said.

"Your new friend is not a friend.
He is a villain named 'The
Bubblegum Bandit!'
To break his lazy spell,
everyone in Bumblyburg
must spit out their gum!"

Alfred's words made Bubba mad.

He began to get bigger and bigger.

"He is blowing up like a bubble,"

said LarryBoy.

"We have to stop him."

He launched his super-suction ear.

The wrinkled, torn suit didn't work.
LarryBoy was stuck to
the bad bubble!

"Everyone spit out your gum,"
Alfred yelled.

As they did, the bubblegum villain
began to shrink.

He got smaller and smaller.

Soon he was nothing

but a wad of gum

stuck to LarryBoy's ear.

"I think it is time to clean my

super suit,"

LarryBoy said with a smile.

Bumblyburg was saved!

Thanks to ... LarryBoy!

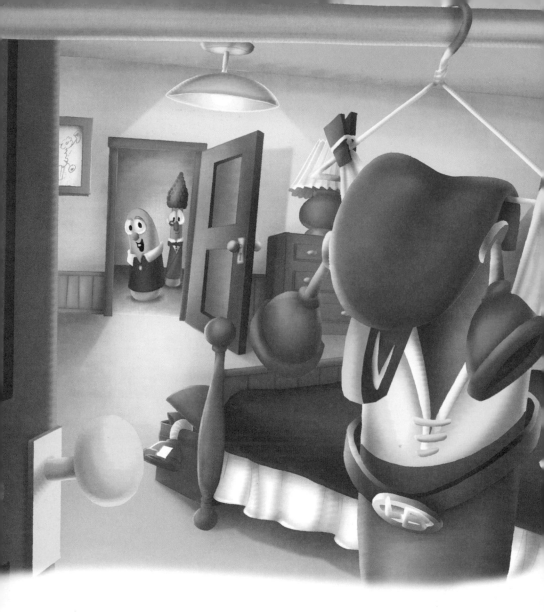

Diligent hands will rule, but
laziness ends in slave labor.

— Proverbs 12:23–25